HECTOR'S HOAX

Get set with a Read Alone!

This entertaining series is designed for all new readers who want to start reading a whole book on their own.

Read Alones may be two or three short stories in one book, or one longer story with chapters, so they are ideal for building reading confidence.

The stories are lively and fun, with lots of illustrations and clear, large type, to make first solo reading a perfect pleasure!

By the same author

HECTOR THE SPECTRE

Some other Read Alones for you to enjoy

CAPTAIN PUGWASH AND THE PIGWIG
  John Ryan
DRAGON RIDE Helen Cresswell
THE GHOST FAMILY ROBINSON
  Martin Waddell
THE GREMLIN BUSTER Rosemary Hayes
LEILA'S MAGICAL MONSTER PARTY
  Ann Jungman
THE LITTLE EXPLORER Margaret Joy
RICKY'S SUMMERTIME CHRISTMAS
  PRESENT Frank Rodgers
THE SLIPPERS THAT TALKED
  Gyles Brandreth

Jana Hunter

Hector's Hoax

Illustrated by Mike Gordon

VIKING

For Alex

VIKING

Published by the Penguin Group
Penguin Books Ltd, 27 Wrights Lane, London W8 5TZ, England
Penguin Books USA Inc., 375 Hudson Street, New York, New York 10014, USA
Penguin Books Australia Ltd, Ringwood, Victoria, Australia
Penguin Books Canada Ltd, 10 Alcorn Avenue, Toronto, Ontario, Canada M4V 3B2
Penguin Books (NZ) Ltd, 182–190 Wairau Road, Auckland 10, New Zealand

Penguin Books Ltd, Registered Offices: Harmondsworth, Middlesex, England

First published 1995
10 9 8 7 6 5 4 3 2 1

Filmset in Monophoto Times New Roman Schoolbook

Made and printed in Great Britain by Butler & Tanner Ltd, Frome and London

A CIP catalogue record for this book is available from the British Library

ISBN 0–670–85469–7

Contents

Have you heard the one about the comic ghost?
He died laughing!

Starring Hector

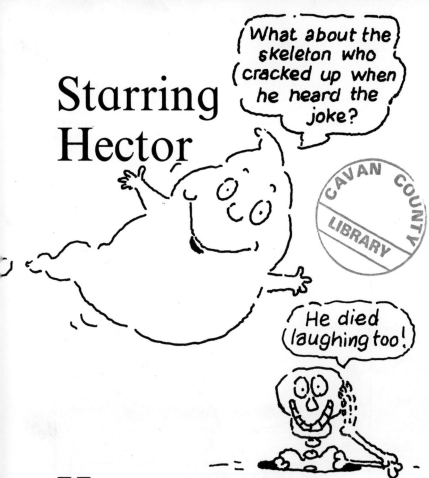

Hector is polishing up his act for the Windy End Talent Contest. It's the best thing in the year at Windy End School . . .

7

. . . and its fame is spreading.

There are singing solos,
dancing duos and of course
the star of the show, Hector
the Spectre. He's the wackiest
wag, the jokiest joker . . .

. . . the most hilarious ghost of all! (His parents would die if they knew.)

Yes, Hector likes to do his
own thing. The funny thing!
Trouble is, he'd like kids
everywhere to enjoy it.

But how can he tell the world about the Windy End Talent Contest?

Telepathy?

Telephone?

TELEVISION!

Brilliant!
I'll pay the studios a flying visit! Teehee...

On the set of Children's Television, it's panic stations. The director, Hans Off, is going bananas.

Something is spooking the guests for today's *Blue Rita* show.

The tortoise who dances a quickstep refuses to come out of her shell . . .

. . . the goat who head-butts a football into goal won't budge . . .

. . . and the man whose collection of novelty rubbers got eaten is calling the police.

No wonder Hans Off is in a
blind panic . . . a blue funk.
The show goes on in an hour.

So Hector helps him out.
He whispers and wheedles . . .

. . . he nudges and needles . . .

. . . he ruffles the newspaper –
until Hans Off can't help
getting the message.

Suddenly, the director orders the camera crew, the lighting crew, the whole crazy lot, to pack up and head for . . . Windy End School!

At the school, the Windy
Enders are thrilled to be
appearing on *Blue Rita*. Even
Ivor Botty, Windy End's
headmaster, can't wait to see
his school on TV.

At last, kids everywhere can
enjoy the talent contest with
the amazing acts.

There's the girl who hangs upside down and recites her two-times table – backwards . . .

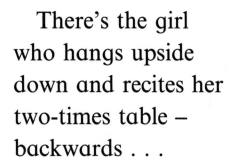

Eight is
two times four,
Six is
two times three,
Four is two twice,
Two is two once.
It's twice as
good upside down!

. . . the kid who can speed-
change into his PE kit while
roller-skating round the hall . . .

. . . and the musical girl who can play a tune with her dinner-money.

It's not surprising that the show is the most successful *Blue Rita* has ever known . . .

. . . or that the biggest success
of all is Hector.

His spirited performance
has kids everywhere howling.
In fact, he's such
an immediate
hit that . . .

. . . letters from kids all over the world pour into the *Blue Rita* studios.

The post room is swamped.

His popularity is more than Hector could ever have dreamed of.

He's fêted and flattered . . .

. . . given the star treatment.

He's even invited to be a
guest on chat shows.

Hans Off is so impressed, he sees his big chance . . .

. . . his chance to have a hit show at last. And Hector is happy to accept.

But the first day on the set,
Hector is given a script . . .

. . . a script without a single
funny line. (And he couldn't
be more disappointed.)

What's more, the lighting technician casts a gloomy shadow over everything . . .

... the sound man wants nothing but groans ...

Groan...I'm the picture of misery. A shadow of my former self

. . . and the camera operator's angle is miserable.

It's clear that Hector's idea
of a show is not the same as
anyone else's in TV.

There's only one thing
for it.

ACTION!

Before you can say "giggling ghosts", Hector has vanished into thin air. While invisible he proves that scaring people is no joke.

43

Now no camera can focus
on Hector's hocus-pocus . . .

. . . no spotlight can beam on
his flight . . .

. . . there isn't a screen can
transmit this being . . .

. . . for he's disappeared from
sight!

At last Hector can make his escape back to his best friends, his most loyal fans of all – the Windy Enders.

Once more Hector's happy –
doing his own thing.

For he knows of all the
shows, COMEDY is king!

Hector's Hoax

Ivor Botty, headmaster of Windy End School, is being driven round the bend.

Not one of his teachers can keep order in the classroom.

Hector and the Windy Enders are more than they can cope with.

It's bad enough teaching unruly kids, but when there's a ghost cracking jokes every time you turn around . . .

. . . . it's a nightmare!

But Hector can't be serious.
He is a ghost who sees the
funny side of everything. And
he likes to cheer things up.
With him the misery of simple
maths simply disappears!

Spelling tests become a
breeze . . .

. . . and Windy End
experiments a gas!

It's enough to make Mr Botty cancel playtime, retire and take up knitting, or . . .

. . . get tough!

Yes, Mr Botty believes it's time the Windy Enders had a shock . . .

. . . a rude awakening.

And he's not the only one (worse luck).

Gilda Glump, ex-tour guide
of Crumblingum Castle,
would love to teach those
Windy End kids a lesson once
and for all.

Since leaving her last job
(due to a nasty experience
involving a ghost and a
tapestry), she hasn't wasted
any time.

In fact, the Glump has been
in training. Not as a wrestler,
nor a sergeant-major, but . . .

. . . as a teacher! Now this human foghorn can't wait to get her hands on the Windy End kids. (She'd love to get her hands on Hector too, but it would be a bit difficult with a ghost.)

Mr Botty is delighted to
give Gilda Glump the job at
Windy End School.

Before you can say "charging rhinos", Gilda Glump has the Windy Enders stunned into silence . . .

. . . and mute with misery.

Though Hector does his best to liven things up, it's hard with the Glump on the warpath.

If he tells a joke or even
chatters in class . . .

. . . the Glump's yells are enough to shatter glass.

If he performs or tries to take centre stage . . .

. . . the Glump storms and
flies into a terrible rage.

It's enough to make a
clown cry.

But with Hallowe'en just around the corner Hector gets an idea. An idea so fantastic that it could not only cheer up everyone, but get rid of the Glump for good.

It's brilliant. It's perfect.
It's . . .

. . . a Hallowe'en party!

Hallowe'en is the one time of year when a ghost can have fun. Trouble is, fun is the one thing Hector's mum and dad don't like.

They'd never throw a party in a million years . . .

. . . unless they think it's a haunt instead of a party. If Hector can fool them into thinking they're having a ghost-gathering, it will be the hoax of the century.

So he begins to work on his parents as only the son of ghosts can.

He moans and surprises . . .

... he groans and materializes ...

. . . he behaves like a holy terror.

Until finally his parents are won round.

The guest-lists are drawn up, and the invitations sent out.

Preparations begin . . .

. . . for the best Hallowe'en
party in Windy End history.

Hector's mum and dad are thrilled at the sight of so many ghosts. Proudly, they show off Hector to those who once despaired of him.

I. Scarem, Hector's old Ghoul School head screecher, just can't get over the change in Hector.

You've done a really good job on Hector. The Spectre Inspector made him scary

What they don't know is
that the screeches and squeals
coming from the top of the
tower are nothing more than
the kids playing Ghostman's
Knock . . .

. . . Pin the Fang on the
Vampire . . .

. . . and Movable Chairs.

Downstairs in the cellar,
only one guest is not fooled.
The Spectre Inspector.

Now when it comes to
happy ghouls, these kids
really pass the test.
As Hector says, "Of all the
schools . . . those that are *fun*
are best!"

. . . *to everyone in town.*

... without Trick or Treat. So
with goody bags in tow, the
Windy Enders make their
rounds . . .

Much to the relief of
Hector's parents, their spirited
haunting is top of the class.

Of course, no Hallowe'en is
ever complete . . .

... the Windy Enders are ready for them. When it comes to ghost games, Hector's schooled them well.

... where, to their undying surprise ...

In a flash, the Inspector and I, Scarem fly up the stairs . . .

The Spectre Inspector can see right through Hector. He remembers when he tried to stop Hector's jokes before. The funny ghost was his most difficult case.